dying to be famous

tanya landman

**WALKER
BOOKS**

First published in Great Britain 2009 by Walker Books Ltd
87 Vauxhall Walk, London SE11 5HJ

2 4 6 8 10 9 7 5 3 1

Text © 2009 Tanya Landman

The right of Tanya Landman to be identified as author of this
work has been asserted by her in accordance with the
Copyright, Designs and Patents Act 1988

This book has been typeset in Slimbach

Printed and bound in Great Britain by Clays Ltd, St Ives plc

British Library Cataloguing in Publication Data:
a catalogue record for this book is
available from the British Library

ISBN 978-1-4063-1462-5

www.walker.co.uk

For Lindsey, who knows all
the words

Actress *Tiffany Webb stared at the morning newspapers and sighed. She'd been photographed leaving an exclusive nightclub at four o'clock in the morning. It was the fifth time this month that her face had been splashed across the front pages.*

It wasn't enough.

But the role she'd just been offered should get her more attention. She'd been chosen to play the part of Dorothy in a stage version of The Wizard of Oz! *The newspapers were full of it. Her agent had said that if she got good reviews she could be on her way to Hollywood. Tiffany smiled to herself. She knew that everything would be perfect, just as long as she had the right help. The show would sell out; she would delight critics and dazzle audiences. They'd be on their feet at the end of every performance, clapping and cheering, with tears in their eyes – she could already taste her triumph.*

What Tiffany didn't know was that someone else was looking at the papers that morning, staring at the photographs with horrid fascination. While Tiffany was indulging in dreams of a golden future, that same person saw a far darker vision of what lay ahead. Tiffany would never play the part of Dorothy. Before the opening night, she would have an accident that would bring her stage career to a sudden and dramatic end.

the reluctant
marigold

My name is Poppy Fields. There are lots of things I like watching. Comedies? Great. Spy thrillers? Brilliant. War films? Dead exciting. But musicals? I just don't get them. All that smiling and dancing and bursting into song for no reason at all? It's weird. The first time I saw one I thought it was just plain silly.

So how did I end up with a huge orange flower stuck on my head, cowering in the dressing room, sick with stage fright among a bunch of Munchkins on the opening night of *The Wizard of Oz*? It certainly didn't have anything to do with liking the limelight. I've never wanted to be famous. Most of the time I try to blend into the background. I've got so good at Not Being Noticed that sometimes my mum, Lili, calls me The Invisible Girl. I'm not shy, it's just that I'm really interested in human behaviour. Studying other people is a bit like being a bird watcher: you have to keep quiet and move carefully so you don't frighten your subjects away.

In normal circumstances I'd never even have considered auditioning for a part in a musical. But these weren't normal circumstances.

Tiffany Webb made sure of that.

She was the star of the TV soap "Dead End Street" but she was as famous for her social life as her acting. She was forever being photographed at all-night parties, or getting arrested for bopping paparazzi or having screaming rows with other celebrities. Her face was constantly in the papers or on the covers of magazines – it seemed like you couldn't walk past a newsagent without seeing a photo of her on *something*. She'd had a series of well-known boyfriends too. When I added them up it came to two film stars, three pop singers, seven footballers and a boxer.

But I wasn't interested in her simply because she was a celebrity – it wasn't the fact that she was famous that I found fascinating. What intrigued me was how *desperate* she was to be noticed. I saw her on TV at an awards ceremony once and she was practically pushing other people off the red carpet. It was like she *had* to be the centre of attention; as if she was scared that she might disappear in a puff of smoke if no one was looking at her. I was working on the theory that publicity was like a mirror: she needed it to prove to herself that she really existed.

I suspected that she was slightly insane, so when I had the opportunity to observe her up close it was irresistible. That was why I ended up in *The Wizard of Oz.*

It was right after the October half-term. The first Monday morning back at school our head teacher, Mr Thompson, made a dramatic announcement in assembly.

"Something rather exciting is going to happen this Christmas," he told us, rubbing his hands together with obvious delight. I thought he was going to tell us about some school disco or a design-a-festive-card competition. I stifled a yawn. But then he said, "Anyone heard of the Purple Parrot Theatre Company? Come on now. Hands up."

He looked expectantly at a sea of blank faces. Hands remained in laps. No one had a clue. No one but Graham, my best friend, whose arm shot up at once. He knows stuff, you see. His head is packed with a mind-blowing assortment of occasionally-fascinating-but-mostly-useless information.

"It's a touring company that specializes in music-als," Graham informed us.

"Good lad, well done," said Mr Thompson, award-ing him a house point while simultaneously looking deeply disappointed with the rest of us. "For those of you who don't know, they're one of the most presti-gious outfits in the UK. They move from town to town, taking their spectacular shows from one venue to the next so you don't have to travel to London to see first-rate theatre. And this Christmas they're bringing their version of *The Wizard of Oz* to our Theatre Royal. What's more, they're looking for local children to play the parts of the Munchkins!"

There was a buzz of anticipation from the kids who liked doing school plays or were part of the choir. Graham and I weren't interested in drama or singing so we didn't share it. I'd kind of switched off by then and I barely heard Mr Thompson saying it was the "opportunity of a lifetime" and that anyone who succeeded in getting a part could have time off school for rehearsals.

But then he mentioned that Tiffany Webb would be playing Dorothy and suddenly I was all ears.

It was my big chance to observe a living celebrity in the flesh and I wasn't going to pass it up without a fight. I mean, I'd had a similar opportunity during half-term when my mum – who's a landscape gardener – was invited to make over the Hollywood estate of a retired actress. Sadly that particular star had gone and got herself murdered before I could study her behaviour. So I was doubly determined to grab this fresh chance with both hands. I had no choice but to audition.

Either side of me and Graham the girls we call the Pink Fairy Brigade began their preening rituals, flicking their hair across their shoulders and checking their nails. If I wanted a part, clearly I would have a lot of competition.

When I told Graham we were going for it, he was less than enthusiastic.

"You can't sing and I can't act," he pointed out. "Statistically speaking, the chances of us being offered a part are a zillion to one."

"It's worth a go, though, isn't it, Graham? What have we got to lose?"

"Dignity. Pride. Self-respect…"

"Come on, it will be fun," I wheedled. And before Graham could start going on about the Very Slim Chances of the Experience Being Even Remotely Amusing, I offered him the best bribe I could think of. I promised to buy him the latest edition of *Guinness World Records* for Christmas. It wasn't enough. I had to throw in an updated *Book of Lists* as well before he agreed.

For the next week we practised singing "Follow the Yellow Brick Road". We even devised a sort of dance routine but I have to admit we were truly terrible. I didn't think we had a hope of getting in.

But on the first Saturday in November we took the bus into town. Clutching the parental consent forms our mums had signed, we joined the back of a queue of Eager Young Hopefuls that wound three times around the Theatre Royal and snaked away over the horizon.

We had to hang around for *hours*: Graham and I were the very last ones in.

I was convinced that the Pink Fairy Brigade and the I'm-going-to-be-an-actor-when-I-grow-up mafia would have grabbed all the singing and dancing parts in the first few minutes. When we finally walked on to the stage, the director – a tall thin man who introduced himself as Peregrine Wingfield – looked about ready to gnaw his own hands off with boredom. We barely got the first word of our song out when he called, "Lovely! That'll do." He turned to a large lady next to him and said wearily, "Cynthia, are *they* the right size?"

Graham and I looked at each other, mystified, as Cynthia ran up to us with a tape measure. "I'm the chaperone. I look after the children in the production," she explained as she measured the circumference of my head. "Perfect!" she muttered to herself before turning to Graham and doing the same to him. "They'll do!" she called back.

"What a relief!" Peregrine sighed. "That's me done for the day, then. I'll be in the bar, Cynthia. See you later." He left the auditorium.

"Right, you two," Cynthia said briskly. "Come with me."

Cynthia sang softly under her breath ("It's a Long Way to Tipperary") as she descended several flights of stairs, Graham and I following obediently behind, all the way down to the basement, where a small room was stuffed with outfits.

It turned out that it was the Purple Parrot Theatre Company's policy to audition *everyone* who turned up. Good for public relations, apparently. But in reality, once they'd cast the singing–dancing Munchkin parts it was down to who would fit into the remaining costumes. Cynthia told us that a load of wonderfully-talented-but-sadly-too-tall/short/wide/weedy kids had already been led away weeping by their disappointed parents.

But I turned out to be just the right size for the Orange Marigold.

Graham was perfect for the Pink Petunia.

It seemed that the person who'd designed the Purple Parrot's production had given Munchkinland an extra special feature. We were destined to adorn the stage as part of a magical herbaceous border. We wouldn't have to sing or dance. All we'd have to do was sit in a corner and wiggle our petals in time with the music.

"I hope you're not too disappointed." Cynthia looked deeply anxious. "The Fantastical Flowers aren't what you'd call demanding roles. You might find it a little dull just watching everyone else do their bit."

"No," I answered honestly as I studied my outfit. Costume? I thought. It's camouflage. It looked as solid as a bird watcher's hide. "This will be perfect," I said, thinking how closely I'd be able to study Tiffany's Celebrity Behaviour.

I had no idea that someone else was already watching Tiffany Webb. Someone who wanted to do her some serious damage.

death threat

The first thing we had to do for the Purple Parrot Theatre Company was what they called "advance publicity". They'd arranged a photo call early on Monday morning to launch the show so, instead of going to school as usual, Graham and I had to catch a bus into town. All the kids were supposed to report to Maggie on the stage door at 8 a.m. sharp so that we could get made up and into the right costumes. By 9.15 a.m. we should have been standing on the broad, stone steps of the Theatre Royal waiting for Tiffany Webb, dressed in her Dorothy outfit, to pull up in a horse-drawn carriage and pose for the flock of photographers and TV crews who'd turned up for the occasion.

Things didn't quite work out according to plan.

First of all, the bus Graham and I were supposed to catch was fifteen minutes late. Then it crawled through the rush-hour traffic so slowly that we didn't get into town until nearly nine o'clock. I was really edgy because I thought we'd be chucked out of the show before we'd even got started and Graham was beside himself because he hated being behind schedule. We sat there, drumming our fingers on the backs of the seat in front of us, jiggling our feet, tutting and sighing, and generally annoying the other passengers.

The area around the theatre was pedestrianized, so, once we'd reached our stop, we had to sprint the last five hundred metres. The quickest way to the stage door was through an alley where the fire escapes crisscrossed the side of the building down to the ground.

When we got there Maggie sent us straight inside. One minute and forty-seven seconds later we were clad in lurid leafy tunics and brightly coloured tights. Cynthia had done our faces to match, singing bursts of "I Can Sing a Rainbow" as she daubed us with garish greasepaint. Cramming the flowers on our heads, she dragged us by our wrists back through the stage door, along the alley and round to the front of the theatre.

"If we go this way Peregrine won't spot you,"

she said. "You can slip in among the Munchkins and he'll be none the wiser."

As we reached the theatre's main entrance, Cynthia shoved us towards the already crowded steps. "Go up the side there. Stand at the back. You'll be fine. Go on."

We did as we were told, squeezing between Munchkins until we reached the top. From there we could see the rest of the cast arranged artfully for the cameras. They were all there: the Tin Man, the Cowardly Lion, the Scarecrow, the Wizard of Oz, Glinda the Good Witch and the Wicked Witch of the West. They were chatting and laughing but then there was the sound of hoofbeats on concrete, and everyone fell into a hushed, expectant silence.

An emerald-green open carriage was being pulled towards us by two pea-coloured ponies. "I wonder how they did that?" I whispered to Graham.

"Coloured hair spray I should imagine," he replied. "It would need to be completely non-toxic."

"Bet those horses didn't like being zapped with green," I said. "They're probably really embarrassed."

"Actually, horses are completely colour-blind," Graham informed me. "But I wouldn't want to be the person who has to wash it off."

And then we fell silent too because all eyes were

on the girl in the gingham frock and ruby slippers. Tiffany Webb. Dorothy. Smiling and waving just like the Queen, only with more enthusiasm and whiter teeth.

She was a lot smaller than I thought she would be and for a second I was slightly disappointed. She looked kind of fragile sitting there all on her own. When the carriage came to a halt the Cowardly Lion bowed and stepped forward to open the door. Suddenly the respectful silence was broken by the frantic clicking and flashing of hundreds of cameras. Photographers were shouting, calling her name to get her attention. "This way, Tiffany!" "Over here, love!" "Give us a smile, darling!" A film crew dangled a fluffy microphone in her face and demanded, "How do you feel about your new role, Tiffany?"

It was worse than being at a wedding. The photographs took forever. They took shots of Tiffany and the other principal actors and then did a load of wide-angle ones of the whole cast standing on the steps. Graham and I were elbowed out of the pictures by pushier, more publicity-hungry kids but neither of us minded. The TV crew did an interview with Tiffany and then a celebrity magazine wanted more pictures of her in the carriage with the green horses. Everyone's eyes were firmly fixed on Tiffany at the bottom of the steps but my attention began to wander. I turned around and it was then that I noticed a wizard edging furtively towards the theatre's front doors.

I prodded Graham.

"What?" he said, a little crossly. Then he saw what I was looking at and his mouth fell open.

I mean, it was quite a sight.

Six, maybe seven feet tall; black flowing cape; pointy hat; bright green warty mask. It was like seeing Darth Vader out trick-or-treating.

"Must be someone from the play," said Graham uncertainly. "Probably here for the photo call."

"Maybe," I replied. "But why isn't he down there with the rest of the actors?"

"I don't know."

"There's only one wizard in *The Wizard of Oz*, isn't there?" I asked.

"Yes," replied Graham. "And he's standing right next to Tiffany."

We watched, and to our horror the tall wizard suddenly pulled a lethal-looking knife from beneath his cape and raised the blade high in the air. With a thud he brought it down hard, stabbing a piece of paper to the front door. Then he ran off down the side of the steps, disappearing into the alley so quickly that we didn't have a chance of stopping him.

The piece of paper flapped helplessly beneath the knife in the breeze. When Graham and I read what was written on it, my blood ran cold. Scrawled in scarlet ink were the words TIFFANY WILL DIE!

the stalker

"**Inspector** Humphries takes threats of this nature very seriously. He has placed Miss Webb under police protection until the suspect is apprehended."

Graham and I watched the evening news wincing with embarrassment as the whole drama replayed across the screen for everyone to see.

I mean, we'd been horrified when we read the note. We were in deep conversation with our backs to everyone else when Tiffany finally ascended the theatre steps on Peregrine's arm, closely followed by the film crew that was recording her every move. We didn't even hear them coming.

In full, glorious technicolour the TV audience was

treated to a close-up of our bright and leafy bottoms. We'd been blocking their way, so Peregrine had coughed loudly. Only then had we turned around.

He hadn't said anything: just fixed us with a steely stare and jerked his head so that we were compelled to stand aside. Then he'd spotted the note and the knife, and chaos had erupted.

Tiffany had gasped and staggered as if she was deeply upset; Peregrine had sworn so violently they'd had to bleep his words out on the news; and Cynthia had called the police.

The TV news froze for a few seconds on a close-up of the note's shocking words. An interview with Tiffany – distressed but courageous – followed.

"Is there anyone you think might be responsible for this?" the interviewer asked sympathetically.

"I really don't know."

"An ex-boyfriend, perhaps?" the interviewer suggested.

"Maybe," Tiffany said.

"Or a crazed fan?"

"I've no idea. I can't think why anyone would want to hurt me. The police are looking into it. They seem to think I might have a stalker."

"And will you alter your plans at all as a result of this threat? Starring in a live theatre show might expose you to danger. Will you go ahead?"

"Of course!" Tiffany threw back her head, raising her chin defiantly. "I've always wanted to play the part of Dorothy. Nothing's going to stop me. He'd have to kill me first." Then she looked right at the camera, as if she was issuing her stalker a direct challenge.

I thought her manner was kind of interesting.

If someone had sent me a note like that there's no way on earth I'd go on stage in front of a live audience. Anyone could take a pot shot at you – it's not like there's bullet-proof glass between you and the punters. Being Dorothy was obviously really important to Tiffany – so important that she'd risk her life to go ahead.

I was fascinated watching that interview. Normally when people talk on the news you can tell they're a bit uncomfortable – they scratch their noses or pull at their ears or pick their nails. They say "erm" and "ah" and trip over their words. They do little things that can tell you what they're really feeling. A touch of panic. A shred of fear. A hint of embarrassment. You can usually see all of those.

But I didn't with Tiffany.

Usually there's a big difference between someone who's acting and someone who's taking part in a reality TV show. However people act in soap operas – however grittily realistic they try to make it – you can tell they're speaking lines someone else has written for them. But with Tiffany there was no difference – she talked in that interview exactly the same way she talked in "Dead End Street". With her you just couldn't work out where the acting ended and the real person began.

When it was over I switched off the TV and said to Graham, "Do you think she looked a bit ... I don't know ... *theatrical*?"

"She's an actress," he pointed out reasonably.

"What do you reckon about this stalker, then?"

Graham paused. "A high proportion of famous actresses acquire a stalker at some time or another. It's often an obsessed fan. They can be very persistent."

"They don't usually dress up, though, do they? Do you think he'd really try to hurt her?"

"From what I've read, I gather that anonymous threats are rarely carried out. The main object of the exercise is to instil fear into one's victim," said Graham wisely.

"Well he's failed there, then," I said. "She's being very brave about it."

Graham frowned. "Let's hope it doesn't drive him to more extreme measures."

The next morning every front page carried headlines like DARING TIFFANY DEFIES DEATH or DEADLY DOROTHY?

or BRAVE TIFFANY RISKS ALL FOR OZ. Everywhere you looked there were photos of her. Whatever the stalker wanted to achieve – whether he meant to kill her or simply scare her – there was no denying that he'd created great publicity for *The Wizard of Oz*. When the box office opened the following morning, the tickets for the whole run sold out in less than an hour.

act one

Tiffany was in London for the rest of that week. While she was busy filming "Dead End Street", her stalker was busy sending her more death threats. We saw her on the news every day. Notes were popping up everywhere: stuck on the reception desk at the TV studios; nailed to the front door of her flat; taped to the seat of the exercise bike in the exclusive gym she frequented. Each time one of the messages appeared there was a corresponding sighting of a masked figure in a wizard's hat and cape – a neighbour had seen him driving away, or the security guard had glimpsed him disappearing around a corner. On one occasion he was caught on CCTV. Inspector Humphries showed me and

Graham the footage so that we could confirm it was the person we'd seen at the theatre. Not that we could be one hundred per cent certain. I told the policeman, "The outfit looks the same all right, but anyone could be underneath that mask, couldn't they?"

Inspector Humphries admitted, "Yes. That's precisely the problem."

In every interview she gave, Tiffany remained brave and defiant, and refused to be terrorized into giving up the part. I suspected that underneath that fragile-looking exterior lurked an iron will.

By trawling through news sites on the Internet, Graham and I kept an eye on the police investigation. They'd interviewed each and every one of her past boyfriends since the first note had appeared. But the two film stars, three pop singers, seven footballers and the boxer didn't seem to be very convincing stalker material to me.

"Really," I complained to Graham when we trawled through a gossipy celebrity site, "when you look at it more closely they hardly count as boyfriends at all."

"What do you mean?"

"Well, look," I pointed at each of them in turn. "As far as I can see, she went to a party with that singer. She had dinner with that actor and lunch with the other one. That footballer took her to Alton Towers and she went to Wimbledon with that one. She went to a polo match with that singer, the races with that one, and a nightclub with him. She went to different award ceremonies with all the other guys. They were just single dates. She went on holiday with the boxer but it was with a huge group of people and there aren't any photos of them alone together. As far as I can see, she didn't have a serious relationship with any of these people. She hasn't been out with anyone long enough for them to get possessive and obsessed."

"You're looking at it too logically," said Graham earnestly. "The true stalker is a delusional obsessive. Some of them never even meet their victims face-to-face and yet they think they're married to them or something stupid."

"Really?"

"Oh yes. They end up believing all kinds of peculiar things. It's called de Clerambault's syndrome, I think. There was one famous case I read about when a woman became fixated on King George V. She thought he was in love with her and used to hang around outside Buckingham Palace. Every time the servants drew the curtains she was convinced he was sending secret signals to her."

I was impressed. "Wow! That's really bonkers."

"Yes. And there was this mad guy in America who

was obsessed with a movie actress. He tried to assassinate the President because he reckoned it would force her to admit she loved him. But she didn't even know he existed!"

"Weird!" I looked back at the computer screen. "So it could be one of her boyfriends then?"

"Possibly. Or it could be a man she's never met."

"It could be a woman too, couldn't it?" I asked, and Graham nodded. "Maybe it's someone she sat next to in the hairdresser's. Or a girl who did her nails."

"Or it could be any one of a million people who've seen her on TV, or passed her in the street," offered Graham.

"Well, in that case it could be anyone at all," I sighed. "How on earth will they ever catch them?"

the read-through

We didn't see Tiffany in the flesh again until the read-through.

It was set for the following Monday, so Graham and I got to miss school again. I'd never taken part in so much as a nativity play before so I wasn't quite sure what to expect. When we reached the theatre, Cynthia herded me and Graham to the side of the stage with the other kids, where we couldn't get in the grown-ups' way. The death threats had made everyone extremely tense, I thought, or maybe it was normal for theatre people to be irritable at the start of rehearsals.

Peregrine was barking instructions at Geoff, the technician, who was lugging chairs onto the stage and setting them down around a long table. Cynthia was minding us kids and humming such a high, fast tune that she sounded like an angry swarm of bees.

Elizabeth, the stage manager, was handing out scripts to the kids and wearing a harassed expression. I took mine and looked at the front cover, where a typed list of characters was set alongside the names of the actors who were playing them.

First there was Dorothy. Tiffany's name was in big block capitals but underneath – in teeny-tiny print – her understudy was listed as Hannah Price. Then there was the Scarecrow (Brad Slater), the Tin Man (Timothy North) and the Cowardly Lion (Rex Butler). These four were the only actors with just one part – the other five had to double up so that, for example, Aunt Em (Belinda Fowler) was also the good witch Glinda, and Uncle Henry (Walter Roberts) got to be the Wizard of Oz too.

I looked around the stage, trying to match up the actors with the names on the script. Rex Butler was standing quite close to me and I could hear the catty conversation he was having with Timothy North and Brad Slater. They were complaining about young actors and their lack of Proper Theatrical Training.

"Television," Rex said, "that's all they're inter-ested in these days. Money for old rope, I say. Call that acting? Five minutes on the box and they think they're stars. The problem with these soap operas is that they're about *ordinary* people. Dull, boring, every-day types. Which is precisely the opposite of what one wants in a musical."

"Lord alone knows how Miss Webb will shape up," sighed Timothy. "She has no experience of live theatre. None whatsoever. Can she sing? Can she dance? I very much doubt it. I can't imagine how they think she'll fill the role."

"Did you hear how much Peregrine is paying her? A small fortune!" grumbled Rex.

Timothy sighed, "And it's not like the company is terribly secure financially, is it?"

"I heard he had to borrow a whole pile of cash to pay for this production," chipped in Brad. "If this doesn't work we could all be out of a job."

"Things aren't what they used to be," moaned Rex.

"Indeed," agreed Timothy.

Tiffany hadn't arrived yet, which was probably just as well given the way her fellow actors were going on about her, but her understudy was there, biting her fingernails in the opposite corner of the stage. When I looked at Hannah I thought I'd never seen anyone who looked less like Dorothy. I mean, she's supposed to be an innocent farm girl from Kansas, but Hannah had dark hair gelled into savage spikes and wore lashings of purple eyeshadow and thick, black lipstick. I heard Cynthia whisper to Rex, "She's a pretty girl underneath all that. Look at that bone structure. I can't think why she wears so much slap."

"My darling Cynthia," he replied in a voice that boomed out of his chest as if he kept a loudspeaker in his vest, "how can we possibly fathom the workings of young people's minds? The youth of today are an utter mystery."

There was an air of breathless anticipation among the kids while we waited for Tiffany to arrive. When she finally swept on to the stage – two bodyguards shadowing her like menacing guardian angels – I happened to be looking at Hannah.

If I hadn't been staring right at her I'd have missed the flash of hatred that contorted the understudy's face. It was only for a second – she got her expression under control almost immediately – and then her features were impassive beneath her mask-like make-up.

I glanced at Tiffany to see if she'd noticed but of course she hadn't. She was scouring the stage for Peregrine and when her eyes fell on him she turned her smile on. It was like a searchlight. Our director received a thousand-watt blast that almost knocked him off his feet. He was instantly besotted. Satisfied with the effect, Tiffany bestowed a smile on the other actors. The Tin Man, Scarecrow and Cowardly Lion were also dazzled by its brilliance. But the lesser actors like Aunt Em and Uncle Henry were given dimmer versions. Hannah was only sent a small, tight grin that didn't even crease Tiffany's eyes and clearly Munchkins and Fantastical Flowers didn't rank highly enough to deserve anything. She looked over our heads as if we weren't there.

Tiffany thumped her huge designer handbag – bright pink with lots of gold buckles and monogrammed with her initials – down in the wings. Then Peregrine introduced her to everyone, including Cynthia, Elizabeth and Geoff, the technician who'd been putting out the chairs. Once they were finished and without further ado, the grown-ups and the kids with speaking parts sat around the table with their scripts in front of them. The rest of us sat on the floor to listen and the read-through began.

It wasn't what you'd call riveting stuff. Although some of the actors – like Rex Butler – really threw themselves into it, making the air vibrate with their ringing voices, some just spoke their lines as if they were saving their energy for later.

Tiffany was one of them. And when she got to the

bit where she was supposed to sing "Over the Rainbow" she gave a little cough and said, "I won't sing just now if you don't mind, Peregrine. I have a slight cough. I don't want to strain my voice." She smiled winsomely and he was powerless to do anything but gape and nod obediently. I glanced at Hannah to see her reaction. She wasn't glaring with hatred at Tiffany, she was doing something far stranger: smirking with a malicious kind of satisfaction. I nudged Graham and jerked my head in Hannah's direction.

"What?" he muttered.

"Hannah looks pleased."

"So she does," said Graham. "Do you think that has some sort of significance?"

"Don't know. It's just a bit weird."

The actors plodded on through the script without anything else happening that was even remotely interesting. We were within one page of finishing – we had nearly reached the bit where Dorothy clicks the heels of her ruby slippers together and says, "There's no place like home" – when Tiffany let out a strange, strangled gasp. Her face went a sickly yellow and her eyes practically popped out of her head.

"Is something wrong?" asked Peregrine anxiously.

"Why can't he leave me alone?" Tiffany whispered. She held up her script and turned it round to show the director. Over his shoulder I could see that the last page had been torn out. And scrawled across the inside back cover in scarlet ink were the words YOU HAVE BEEN WARNED!

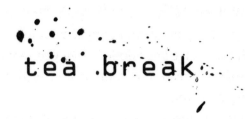

tea break

There was a big, dramatic pause and then everyone burst out talking. "Her stalker!" "That's got to be the same guy!" "But how did he manage to...?" "How could he...?"

Peregrine cut through the rising hubbub of voices. "Keep calm, everyone, I'm sure we can get to the bottom of this. Perhaps it's just someone's silly idea of a joke. Geoff, would you go and ring the police? They ought to be informed." He turned to Elizabeth. "Darling, when did you give Tiffany her script?"

"She asked for an advance copy. I posted it out to her agent two weeks ago," Elizabeth replied.

"And did you check it through beforehand?" Peregrine asked.

"Well, no," confessed Elizabeth. "It never occurred to me that anyone would tamper with it."

"It can't have been done before you sent it," Tiffany said softly. "I read it as soon as it arrived. I wanted to be prepared, you know?"

"Very commendable," soothed Peregrine. "When did you last look at it?"

Tiffany frowned. "Let me see... Yesterday, I think. Yes. I read it through in bed. But I fell asleep before I got to the end."

"So it could have been tampered with before then?" he asked.

Tiffany nodded. "Yes. I've been carrying it around with me since I got it. It was all right in the morning because I looked through it before I went out for lunch with my agent. But the restaurant was very crowded. I suppose anyone could have slipped it out of my bag."

Peregrine looked around at the assembled cast. He was clearly thinking the same as I was – that anyone in the theatre could have done it. I mean, she'd left her bag in the wings while Peregrine had been doing the introductions. While she'd been dazzling everyone with her high-voltage smile someone could have grabbed her script. It would have been difficult to scrawl on it without being noticed: difficult, but not impossible.

So we were all suspects. The thought seemed to occur to everybody at once. Suddenly we were eyeing each other up nervously. Everyone that is except Hannah, who was staring at the floor, and Rex, who was regarding Tiffany with ill-concealed disdain.

"Tea," said Cynthia briskly. "That's what we need. Strong, sweet tea. It's good for shock."

"Oh, yes please," said Tiffany weakly. "That would be wonderful. I left my cup in the green room on the way in. It's the one with my initials on." It was just as well she was sitting down because she looked quite faint.

A few minutes later Cynthia's singing ("Tea for Two") signalled the return of her and Geoff. Both were carrying trays stacked high with tea for the grown-ups, orange squash for the kids and biscuits for everyone. Geoff started to rip open the packets and hand them round. There was a bit of a scuffle for the chocolate ones. The plain wholewheats got left on the table.

Tiffany fetched her bag and groped around inside for her sweeteners. She dropped a couple into her mug – an elaborate pink creation with TW painted in gold on the side – and I noticed how badly her hands were shaking as she stirred her tea. She was trying hard not to show it, but Tiffany was very upset. In fact she was so rattled that when Geoff offered her a biscuit she jumped about a metre in the air and knocked the cup he was holding out of his hands. Scalding hot tea splashed all down his front.

"I'm so sorry!" Tiffany gasped, frantically dabbing at his shirt with a tissue from her bag. "How awful! Here, you'd better have mine." Flushed with embarrassment, she thrust her full mug into his hand. "I'll go and make myself another."

She leapt up and ran off to the green room so quickly that her bodyguards had to sprint across the stage like a pair of bulky shadows.

Geoff watched Tiffany leave then started on her tea. Once he'd drained the last dregs from Tiffany's cup, he put it down. Two seconds later, he was clutching at his throat and his face had turned a violent shade of purple. There was this ghastly wheezing noise as he struggled for breath. And then he collapsed, crashing onto the table, smashing the cups and saucers, and crushing the unpopular packets of plain biscuits. Cynthia was screaming for someone to do something, but before anyone could even ring for an ambulance, Geoff was dead.

the stalker's
mistake

We didn't get any more rehearsing done that day. People were too gripped by the real-life drama to even think about acting. Besides, the police wanted to take detailed statements about exactly who had been doing what, when and where. No one was allowed to leave the building until they'd finished, so we had a long afternoon ahead of us.

Graham and I had seen a few corpses in our time but we'd never had anyone poisoned right in front of us like that. We were both pretty shaken. Everyone was. It was now blindingly obvious that Tiffany's stalker hadn't been making empty threats – he really did want her dead. When Geoff was carried away on a covered stretcher, Tiffany's lower lip started wobbling. You could almost see the thought bubble floating above her head that if she hadn't spilt his tea it would have been her lying there with a sheet over her face.

What was less clear was how the poison had got into her cup.

"It must have been one of us!" Cynthia cried dramatically after Geoff's body was removed from the building. "Somebody here, on the stage, right now."

"Oh I don't think so! No! Surely not!" protested Tiffany, looking around at everyone.

"A stranger couldn't have got in," insisted Cynthia. "Maggie wouldn't have let anyone through the stage door!"

"But the fire escape was open when I went to make another cup of tea," said Tiffany. "Didn't you notice?"

Cynthia blinked and looked at her. "Was it?"

Tiffany nodded.

"Well, yes…" Cynthia frowned as she tried to remember. "I suppose it must have been. I wondered where the draught was coming from. The stalker must have put the poison in your tea when I went to ask Geoff to help me carry the trays. It's so awful!"

Awful as it was, Cynthia visibly relaxed. Everyone did. The prospect of having a killer in the theatre was too much to bear. Before they started talking to the cast and crew, the police examined the fire escape door and confirmed it had been jemmied open from the outside. So everyone in the theatre seemed to be Off the Hook.

The police began by interviewing Tiffany in her dressing room. We were allowed off the stage into the auditorium, where at least the chairs were comfy. The shock of Geoff's death suddenly hit Cynthia like a sledgehammer. One minute she was crooning "We'll Meet Again" to herself and the next she was crying her eyes out while Elizabeth – who was looking pretty near the edge too – patted her arm helplessly. In between convulsive, snorting sobs Cynthia wailed, "Poor Geoff. He was retiring next year. What will his wife do now? They were planning to go on a cruise. Oh dear. It's too ghastly!"

"It is," agreed Peregrine. "He was a good man as well as a good technician. We're going to miss him."

"A premature exit. A role cut short. It's utterly tragic," sighed Rex.

I listened to the grown-ups talking while my brain ticked over. Personally, I wasn't convinced about the fire escape and said so to Graham.

"There are stairs all up the side of the building," he said, shaking his head. "It would be easy for someone to get in that way."

"But the door could just as easily have been opened from the inside," I replied.

"It's a valid theory," he conceded.

I combed my fringe down over my eyes and peered out from under it, examining each and every face in the rows of seats. Most people looked worried, or tearful, or shocked, or a combination of all three. One or two of the kids were actually quite excited – they didn't know Geoff personally and having him drop dead was pretty sensational. Nothing like that had ever happened to them before and their eyes were shining with the unexpected thrill of it. Peregrine's face had gone grey and his hands were shaking while he tried to make notes on his script. Timothy and Brad looked pretty rattled but Rex was beginning to look more bored than upset. He gave a big yawn and complained to no one in particular, "All this hanging around waiting. It's worse than being on a film set."

As for Hannah: she didn't seem to be suffering from any excess of grief but she was certainly troubled. She was sitting four seats away from us with a newspaper across her lap that was open at the Sudoku page. Her forehead was creased into a frown as if she was concentrating hard and every so often she'd fill in one of the boxes in the square grid.

Eventually it was our turn to be interviewed by the

police. Graham and I got up and edged down the row of seats to where Cynthia was waiting to accompany us. Hannah had her legs stretched right out and her bag was blocking the way. She moved so we could squeeze past her and it was then that I glanced down at her paper. With a prickle of unease I noticed that she hadn't been writing down numbers at all.

She'd filled all the boxes of the puzzle with tiny little skulls.

"The show must go on." That's what Peregrine told us just before we were finally allowed to go home. "Tiffany is absolutely determined to go ahead," he said, holding out his hand to his leading lady. She took it and gave him one of her scared-but-determined smiles. "And I wholeheartedly support her. This production must succeed." I noticed that his eyes had taken on a slightly fanatical gleam.

"Told you he was worried about money," Rex muttered to Timothy out of the corner of his mouth. "He can't afford a flop."

"He's got too much at stake," Timothy hissed back.

"We can't let one crazed madman stop us doing our job," declared Peregrine to his cast and crew. "Geoff wouldn't have wanted that. The police are stationing men right here in the building so we'll all be perfectly safe. There's no way on earth the stalker will get in again, I have Inspector Humphries' personal guarantee of that. We'll call it a day now – you can return to your homes. But be back here bright and early tomorrow morning. I expect to see you at 8.30 a.m. sharp to start blocking."

"What's blocking?" I whispered to Graham.

"No idea," he said. "I suppose we'll find out."

Blocking turned out to be extremely tedious.

What happened was that Peregrine told everyone where to stand and when to move, and the actors read out their lines. We had to walk through the basic dance moves without the music and everyone had to scribble things down on their scripts so they'd remember what to do next time. It was all very slow and boring. Of course, Graham and I didn't have to do much more than sit at the back of the stage so after an hour I was beginning to wish I'd paid more attention to him and we'd never auditioned in the first place.

But then Jason turned up and things started to get interesting.

the new technician

Jason Cotton was Geoff's replacement and he was panicking. He burst on to the stage looking tight with stress and immediately started gabbling at Peregrine: "Sorry I'm late! I know I was supposed to get here first thing but my stupid car wouldn't start and then it did but of course I got stuck in traffic and then the wretched Sat Nav sent me down a one-way street by mistake and when I finally got here I couldn't find anywhere to park – it was a complete nightmare!"

Peregrine said, "Never mind, you're here now. And we're only blocking at the moment." But the soothing words didn't quite match his facial expression – he looked cross and Jason seemed well aware of it.

"It won't happen again," he mumbled.

"Tsk, tsk," Rex whispered to Cynthia. "Not a good start on his first day."

"Poor boy," she said. "He's been trying to get a job with the company for weeks. He's been ever so persistent. I do hope he's not going to mess it up."

Jason seemed absolutely determined to compensate for being late. He unzipped a huge holdall and started pulling out cables, speakers and microphones.

Without a word he dashed over to Tiffany and tried to clip a tiny black mike to her lapel. Before he'd even got a hand on her collar her bodyguards shot out from the wings to protect her. The speed with which they moved was really quite impressive.

"It's OK guys," Tiffany said, batting them away. "I'm sure Mason is trustworthy."

"Jason," he corrected her.

"Jason," she repeated. "Sorry." She must still be bothered by what had happened the day before, I thought. I mean, Jason was quite good-looking but she didn't attempt to dazzle him with one of her smiles. Instead she was chewing her lip, staring into space. She didn't even glance at him as he clipped a microphone on each of her lapels. As far as she was concerned he didn't exist.

Jason moved on to Aunt Em and Uncle Henry.

He did the Cowardly Lion, the Scarecrow and the Tin Man. In a few minutes he'd clipped teeny-tiny mikes onto the chests of all the grown-up actors.

Peregrine seemed a bit impatient. "Hurry it up, boy," he said.

But Jason wasn't going to be rushed. "I'd like to get the sound system sorted as soon as I can but it's going to be difficult to get the right acoustic balance in an old theatre like this. It might take me a while to work it out."

"Very well," sighed Peregrine. "Do what you must."

Rex muttered to Cynthia, "In my day we used our diaphragms to project our voices. We had no need of technology." He pronounced "technology" as if it was a filthy swear word and looked with disgust at the microphone clinging to his collar. "That's the problem with employing television actors. They don't know how to use their voices." He carried on moaning for quite some time but I stopped listening to him, because when Jason reached Hannah, something odd happened.

As he walked towards her she took a tiny step back, then half turned as if she had a sudden impulse to run away. It was only for a millisecond and the next moment she was standing still, chin up as if she was confronting him. "I'm only the understudy," she told him briskly. "I won't need a mike."

"Oh," he said, "OK," and moved on to the speaking Munchkins.

Jason showed absolutely no sign whatsoever of recognizing Hannah. There wasn't even a faint glimmer of anything in his eyes. I would happily have bet all my pocket money that he'd never met her before.

But I was equally sure that she knew him.

"That's strange," I said to Graham.

"Yes," he replied. But it turned out that Graham's mind was running on a completely different track to mine. "I always thought theatres had good acoustics, especially old ones," he said, puzzled. "They were built to magnify the human voice. I don't understand why everyone has to have microphones. And why's Tiffany got two? I wonder what kind of amplification system Jason's using?"

I didn't bother answering him. I thought he was being fantastically boringly nerdy. I wasn't remotely interested in technical stuff. But that was a big mistake: if I'd paid more attention to Graham another murder might have been prevented.

murderous munchkins

It wasn't until much later that morning that we finally got to hear Tiffany sing.

By then we'd worked out the basic moves for the first section and Peregrine said that right after the tea break he wanted to do it all again, this time with music. "At this early stage I expect it to be more of a stagger than a walk-through," he said. "But it will at least give us a sense of the direction we're heading in."

His words were greeted with an expectant buzz of chatter and even I felt quite excited.

Tiffany went off to her dressing room "to mentally compose herself" and "get into character" but everyone else stayed on the stage. While the grown-ups drank tea and scoffed biscuits they also did a lot of whispering in a lot of corners. I had a glass of orange squash in one hand and my script in the other – open, as if I was trying to memorize it. As I wandered about casually I managed to overhear a few snatches of muttered conversations.

There was a whole load of not-very-generous speculation from Brad, Timothy and Rex about whether Tiffany's voice would be any good. Hannah didn't say anything, but she sniggered nastily when Rex said he "fully expected our star to have the vocal quality of a rusty harmonica".

Elizabeth wasn't catty but she looked anxious when she told Cynthia, "I do hope Tiffany's going to be good enough. She had a dreadful cold when Peregrine auditioned her. He had to take her agent's word for it that she could sing."

I studied our director for a second. He was sitting bolt upright in the front row of the stalls and sipping his tea – "no milk, just a slice of lemon" – from a bone china cup. His face looked perfectly calm but his shoulders had risen to just below his ears and were a dead giveaway: he was a worried man.

Interesting, I thought. Very interesting.

After the break we started the show from the beginning. Pretty soon we'd reached the scene when

Dorothy's sitting alone on stage. Us kids were crammed into the wings ready to come on when the house gets carried to Munchkinland.

As the opening chords of "Over the Rainbow" struck up I glanced across at Hannah. She was staring fixedly at Tiffany, her black-lipsticked mouth twisted into a grimace of undiluted spite. She was literally licking her lips in anticipation as Tiffany opened her mouth and drew in a breath.

A sweet, pure sound electrified the stage and filled the auditorium. When Tiffany sang it made goose-bumps ping up all over my arms. It wasn't just that she hit the right notes – she filled them with such sad longing that it cut right through me and brought tears to my eyes. It was amazing.

"The voice of an angel," Cynthia muttered. "Oh, I wish poor Geoff had been here to listen. He would have loved it!"

Everyone was utterly awestruck by her performance. Well, nearly everyone. Rex, Brad and Timothy looked extremely disappointed: they'd banged on so much about how TV actors couldn't perform on the stage that it must have annoyed them to be proved wrong.

But if they were cross, Hannah was incandescent.

When Tiffany had started the song, Hannah's jaw

had dropped and her heavily mascaraed eyes had grown wide. But her reaction quickly moved from astonishment to shock and then to confusion. By the time Tiffany had finished singing – to a spontaneous burst of applause from the rest of the cast and wildly enthusiastic congratulations from Peregrine – Hannah's expression had changed again. I'd never seen anything so clearly written on anyone's features.

Hannah was feeling positively murderous.

At lunch time, when I was coming back from the toilets, another odd thing happened. Hannah and Rex were in the corridor behind the stage and no one else was about. As I got nearer I caught a snippet of their conversation.

"Are you quite sure?" Rex demanded. His hands were on Hannah's shoulders and he was staring intently into her face.

"Positive," she said.

"Good heavens! Who would have believed it?"

When they saw me they sprang apart and didn't say anything else. I don't suppose I'd have thought any more about it if they hadn't looked so guilty. And the fact that they'd been standing so close together was odd too: it was like they knew each other really well. Yet on stage they'd always behaved like perfect strangers.

* * *

By the afternoon we'd reached the first big dance routine: the one where Dorothy's house crash-lands and she heads off along the yellow brick road towards the Emerald City. Graham and I had originally been told by Cynthia that all we'd have to do was sit and waft from side to side but it turned out to be more complicated than that. Even though we were plants and therefore should – in theory – have been rooted to the spot, we were supposed to get up and twirl full circle three times on three separate occasions during the song. It took a fair bit of concentration to do it without getting our limbs entwined but we managed without a fuss, which was a lot more than could be said for the Munchkins.

I've never seen so many kids trying so hard to outdo each other. Once the music started they all wanted to sing louder, smile brighter and dance better than anyone else. Everyone was desperate to be *noticed*. The girls put in their own little twirls and flounces with each step, and the boys ended up elbowing each other out of the way so they could be at the front. When a fist fight broke out among the male Munchkins, Tiffany got knocked backwards and ended up sitting in the flower bed with me and Graham. She wasn't hurt but Jason ran in from the wings completely freaked. I thought he was worried about Tiffany but after he'd helped her up he had a major hissy fit, shrieking at us kids about the sensitivity of the sound equipment and how much it would cost to replace anything that got broken.

It was too much for Graham's nerdy curiosity. When Jason paused to draw breath Graham put his hand up as if we were still at school and said, "Excuse me. I've always understood theatre equipment to be remarkably robust. Could you tell me which system you're using?"

Jason turned red but didn't answer. Luckily we were spared a detailed account of the technical complexities by Peregrine impatiently waving Jason off the stage. "Let's get on shall we? We've a lot to get through."

Peregrine had to do a whole load of shouting to make the kids work together that afternoon. "You're a team," he kept yelling. "Not a collection of prima donnas. You're here to support Tiffany, not upstage her."

Only Graham and I did exactly as we were told. We followed the instructions to the letter – did the floral thing with no twiddly bits, no extra steps, no arguing. It was on account of this – Peregrine called it our Solid Professional Approach – that we ended up getting extra roles. To audible sighs of disgust from the other kids, Peregrine announced that he'd chosen us to be the flying monkeys in the second half. We would kidnap Dorothy and whisk her away to the witch's castle.

I was madly excited about it. It would be the ideal opportunity to observe Tiffany close up. We'd be right in the thick of things and I'd really get to find out what made her tick.

But Graham was less thrilled. "Do you know what the likelihood is of us both getting irreversible muscular strain?" he asked. "I read somewhere that flying in a stage harness is physically very demanding. We could be damaged for life."

"You have to suffer for art," I told him. "You ought to be pleased. The other kids would kill for these parts. Did you see their faces? They looked vicious."

I didn't realize anyone was listening until two heavy hands landed on our shoulders, fingernails digging in like claws, and Rex boomed, "Darlings, you have the envy of your fellows to contend with. Such is the price of success. And as if that's not enough, you also run the risk of falling in the path of Tiffany's insane stalker." There was a faint trace of menace in his voice when he added with a smile, "If you two survive until opening night, it will be a miracle."

the yellow brick road

There were plenty of police on duty around the theatre after Geoff's death, so no one saw anything of the mysterious stalker and no death threats arrived. Inspector Humphries seemed convinced that the stalker had been scared off, at least temporarily. But I still wasn't sure it was an outside job. There were so many odd things going on in the theatre that I suspected anyone could be behind it.

Rex and Hannah had been avoiding each other since I'd seen them having that snatched conversation. But I felt Rex's eyes on me a lot of the time, as if he was watching my every move. Hannah had stopped trying to hide how much she hated Tiffany: she just spent her time glaring at the star from the wings. Peregrine on the other hand seemed utterly besotted. He couldn't praise Tiffany enough.

"He seems to be really obsessed with her," I said to Graham at one rehearsal. "Do you reckon he might be her stalker?"

"No... It wouldn't make sense," he objected.

"But you said yourself stalking is a bonkers thing to do. Peregrine's worried about money, isn't he, according to Rex and that lot? Might that be enough to unhinge him?"

Neither of us could come up with a good answer to that question.

Then there were Timothy, Rex and Brad to keep an eye on. Not to mention Walter Roberts who played the part of the Wizard and Uncle Henry. OK, so they were each old enough to be Tiffany's dad but they'd all been at the receiving end of her smile: any one of them might be secretly in love with her.

Christmas was looming. The shops were full of tinselly displays and tinnily piped carols, and the high street's fairy lights had been officially switched on by the mayor. It was late November and we had about two weeks to go before opening night.

Graham and I were kept pretty busy watching

everyone while rehearsals progressed. Once the actors had learnt their lines and knew their moves, Peregrine started working on the finer details like pace and rhythm. It was then that things began to get tricky.

We were practising the bit where the tornado has blown the farmhouse over the rainbow (a neat piece of theatrical engineering involving a load of wires and pulleys). In the blackout we'd all rushed on to the stage to take our places before it landed with a thud, squishing the Wicked Witch of the East flat as a cowpat. The "Ding Dong the Witch is Dead" routine went smoothly. To Peregrine's enormous relief the singing–dancing Munchkins had stopped trying to outdo each other and were working nicely as a team.

But during "Follow the Yellow Brick Road" we got into difficulties.

"The pace is a little slow," said Peregrine, cutting in after the first verse. "The piece needs a lift at this point. Tiffany, darling, your performance is exquisite but I wonder if you'd mind speeding up just a fraction?"

Tiffany nodded obediently. Everyone took their places for the beginning of the number and then Tiffany did it exactly the way she'd done it before.

Peregrine interrupted halfway through. "That's lovely, darling. But we need to shift it along here with just a touch more energy. A little more zest, please, OK?"

"Of course," she said. Everyone got into position. And then she did it again. And again it was just the same as before.

After his seventh interruption Peregrine gave up because each time Tiffany made us go back to the beginning of the song, and took ages and ages to get going again. She stood there taking deep breaths, composing herself. She said she was *feeling* the part, getting into *character*.

I'd read somewhere that lots of actors have weird routines to ward off bad luck. They're a really superstitious bunch. They wear lucky socks, or turn around three times before they go on, or walk through the stage door backwards with their fingers crossed. Tiffany had this funny habit of glancing up and twitching her little finger just before she started singing. It was quite interesting to start with, but as the day wore on even I was beginning to find watching Tiffany tedious.

The rest of the cast were getting short-tempered and some of the kids were tired and starting to make mistakes.

About an hour before home time the Mayor of Munchkinland lost it completely, tying his feet in knots and tripping over Glinda's skirt. Tiffany ground to a halt. Peregrine sighed and said, "Let's just skip ahead to the last verse shall we?"

It was only for a moment. I don't think anyone else even noticed. Peregrine certainly didn't. But in a tiny flash I saw more fear in Tiffany's eyes than I'd seen when Geoff had dropped dead and she knew for certain her stalker wanted to kill her. Something had really terrified her.

Then she threw one of her zillion-volt smiles at Peregrine and said smoothly, "I'd prefer to go back to the beginning, Peregrine. I do so want to get the flow of the piece right. It's terribly important, don't you agree?"

He was powerless to resist – he went all still and frozen like a rabbit caught in the headlights. "Oh yes," he said, nodding so fervently that the hair brushed across his bald patch came adrift and hung down the side of his face like a shower curtain.

This time we managed to get through the whole song – at Tiffany's pace – but by the end of it we were *exhausted*.

"We're never going to get to the Emerald City at this rate," Graham complained as we left.

I was so wiped out that I forgot my lunchbox. We were halfway to the bus stop before I remembered and we had to turn back.

* * *

Empty theatres are spooky places. It must be to do with all that highly charged emotion seeping into the walls with every performance. You could almost believe they're haunted.

I was glad Graham was with me when Maggie let us in through the stage door. We had to go along the echoing corridors past the kids' dressing rooms and then the grown-ups' ones, where someone was having a shower and singing their head off. We couldn't quite make out where the noise was coming from but it was tuneless. Awful.

"They sound worse than you do," said Graham, flashing one of his blink-and-you-miss-it grins.

"Thanks a lot."

We walked on, the caterwauling following us as we climbed a flight of stairs and on to the stage. My lunch-box was at the back where I'd left it. As I retrieved it, I heard a faint click high above me and peered up.

Directly overhead was the grid from which hundreds of massive theatre lights were suspended. During rehearsals when they were switched on you were blinded if you so much as glanced heavenwards. But now they were off and when I looked up I glimpsed a shadowy figure.

Like I said, empty theatres are spooky places. For a moment I thought it was the stalker and I was so terrified I dropped my lunchbox. But when the figure called down to us I realized it was only Jason.

"What are you two doing here?" he demanded rudely.

"I forgot this," I replied, picking the box back up and waving it about as proof. The distant sound of the terrible singing echoed eerily across the stage.

"Oh right," he snapped angrily. "You had better go now. Go on, get out. You shouldn't be here after hours. Health and safety would have a fit."

We turned to leave but before I entirely disappeared into the wings I peeked over my shoulder. Jason hadn't moved. He was watching to make sure we left.

I couldn't see his expression, but I couldn't help wondering why he was so keen to see the back of us.

lethal confection

The next day, Graham and I arrived at the theatre at the same time as a massive bunch of flowers and the biggest box of chocolates I'd ever seen. The man delivering them didn't seem to have arms that were quite long enough to carry both packages. Maggie pressed the buzzer and the stage door swung open to admit us.

"You kids going in?" gasped the struggling delivery man.

"Yes."

"Do us a favour and take these, will you? They're for Miss Webb."

"Sure," I said brightly. "I'll take the chocolates. Graham can carry the flowers, can't you, Graham?"

The opportunity to call at Tiffany's dressing room – maybe even get a peek inside – was too good to miss. Two minutes later we were handing over the gifts to the sweetly smiling actress. She flung her door wide open and told us to come in. Squeezing between the bodyguards stationed in the corridor, we obeyed.

I was slightly unnerved by the smiling. I mean, she'd pretty much ignored me and Graham right the way through rehearsals even though we were the ones who did the flying scene with her. Maybe she was just in a better mood. Or maybe it was the flowers that did it. She took them from Graham, saying, "Lilies! How wonderful. You know some people don't like these – they associate them with funerals. But I think they're beautiful. I love them so much. Aren't they gorgeous?" Peering into the middle of the bunch she pulled a card out and opened it. "*From your biggest fan*," she read aloud. "I wonder who that could be?"

"A secret admirer?" I suggested.

"I suppose so. I've certainly got plenty of those." She put the lilies in the sink, filled it with water and then beckoned me over. "Chocolates, too! Must be an early Christmas present. I wonder if they're from the same person?"

She opened the card that was stuck on the box. "*Sweets to the sweet*. How lovely!" Sitting down, she started to pull off the lid. "My favourites!" she said with a dazzling smile at us both. "I usually go for the soft centres but I fancy a toffee for a change." Popping it into her mouth she held the box out towards us. "I'll eat them all if you don't help me, and that would be terrible for my figure. You'd better save me. Go on, take one."

Graham reached into the box and lifted out a strawberry-shaped one. I picked one in the shape of an orange segment. I was watching Graham, and for some reason the hairs on the back of my neck suddenly stood bolt upright. He lifted the chocolate to his lips and opened his mouth, but just before he put it in I lashed out at him, smacking his hand away so hard that he yelped and both our sweets fell to the floor.

"What did you do that for?" he asked, startled.

"I don't know," I replied. I'd reacted instinctively and it was taking my brain a few minutes to catch up with my body. "Something's not right."

Tiffany's eyes widened. "What do you mean, not right?" She'd already swallowed her toffee. There was a tremble of fear in her voice.

"You don't think there's anything wrong with them, do you?" Graham asked, turning the box over. "Are they past their sell-by date? Even if they are, the risk of contamination is very low. Hardly anyone gets food poisoning from chocolates."

"Food poisoning?" echoed Tiffany. "I don't understand…"

"Poisoning." I turned the word over thoughtfully. Tea… Geoff… A crazed stalker… Lilies… Funeral flowers… It all seemed to fit.

"You don't think…?" gasped Tiffany. "No, it's impossible! You can't really believe they've been tampered with?"

"I don't know. But there's no name on those cards, is there? How do you know they're from a fan? They might be from whoever's been stalking you."

I thought Tiffany was going to pass out. She shut her eyes and leaned back in her chair. Graham firmly replaced the lid on the box. I opened the dressing room door and her minders came bounding into the room ready to repel attackers.

They called the police and the chocolates were taken away for tests. To be honest, it seemed a bit overcautious because Tiffany had eaten hers and she was fine. Even so, when Inspector Humphries came in to talk to us we carefully avoided telling him how close Graham and I had come to eating any. If there *was* something wrong with them he'd tell our mums, they'd freak out and we'd have to stop doing the show. We were far too interested in what was going on for that to happen, so we kept quiet and Tiffany did the same.

After we'd all talked to the inspector, Tiffany was so upset that she had to lie down. Graham and I walked up to the stage and joined the rest of the cast, who were standing in small groups muttering. Word had quickly got around about the suspicious chocolates and the whole place was buzzing with rumours. I sidled nonchalantly up to where Rex and Timothy were talking to Brad.

"Will Tiffany pull out, do you think?" Timothy asked Rex.

"No idea, darling. But I hope Peregrine's got her properly covered."

"What do you mean?" asked Brad.

"Look at it this way," explained Rex. "If he's got her insured and she cops it at least the company won't go under."

At that point Rex noticed me listening and they fell silent. But it gave me something else to think about. Exactly how rocky were the finances of the Purple Parrot Theatre Company? Was it really in danger of collapse? And how far would Peregrine be prepared to go to save it?

We couldn't start rehearsing without Tiffany and she was in a state of shock. But just when it looked like Peregrine would have to give up on the idea of working that day and send us home, our leading lady stepped on to the stage. "I'm not going to let it get to me," she said.

"Bravo!" cried Cynthia. "That's the spirit."

"Besides," Tiffany carried on, "we don't know for sure the chocolates were poisoned. Until we do, I refuse to worry about it." There she stood – brave, defiant and vulnerable. You couldn't help admiring her. And the men couldn't help wanting to protect her. Even Graham looked a bit misty eyed. She was the perfect plucky heroine.

So why did I feel uneasy?

I thought about it all morning while we rehearsed our flying monkey scene. It was my favourite bit of the whole show, even though the costumes Cynthia helped Jason clamp us into (singing "Come Fly with Me" under her breath) were a bit hot and itchy. I mean, synthetic fur's never going to be comfortable, unless you're a stuffed toy. But climbing up onto a tower in the wings and then swooping off in a great arc across the stage was brilliant. Graham thought it was fun too and the other kids were positively green with envy. When we landed we had to scare off Dorothy's dog, Toto, who obliged by yapping very loudly, and then grab her and fly back. Tiffany was wearing a harness too so, despite Graham's gloomy predictions about us getting irreversible muscle strain, it was really easy.

As Jason disconnected us from our harnesses I sneaked a look at Tiffany's profile. I couldn't put it into words: it was too vague. But there was definitely something odd about her. It was to do with what I'd noticed when she was giving the TV interview – the way that you couldn't quite see the gap between when she was being normal and when she was acting. I found it a bit disturbing but when I mentioned it to Graham later he just shrugged and said, "First you thought Hannah was behaving strangely and now it's Tiffany? Maybe they're both stressed. It's a scientifically proven fact that people react with unpredictable emotions when they're under pressure."

Yet Tiffany didn't seem unpredictable when she was on stage – if anything she was just the opposite. When Cynthia (humming "You're the Cream in my Coffee") brought Tiffany her cappuccino, she sighed admiringly.

"Your voice is wonderful," Cynthia said, handing her the cup. "I'm terribly jealous. You never change, you never stumble, you never falter. You're so *consistent*. How on earth do you do it?"

Hannah was close by and her eyes narrowed shrewdly as she waited for Tiffany to respond.

For a second Tiffany looked outraged, almost as if Cynthia had insulted her. But then she did one of those gleaming smiles, which hit Cynthia like a thunderbolt.

"Hard work," Tiffany said. "That's all it is. I'm a professional. I never stop practising."

If Tiffany *was* under terrible pressure like Graham thought then it was certainly greater by the end of the day, when the results came back from the lab. All the soft-centred chocolates – the ones she'd said were her favourites – had been injected with a lethal dose of poison. If Graham had eaten the strawberry one he wouldn't be with us any more, he'd be in hospital. Or the mortuary: dead on a slab in a fridge right next to Geoff. And I'd be there with both of them. It made me feel quite dizzy but Graham seemed a lot less bothered about it than I was.

"The reality is that we avoid death several times a day," he said with one of his blink-and-you-miss-it grins as we left the theatre. "Every time you cross the road you risk fatal injury. There's no point fretting about what might have happened."

The story was all over the evening news. We watched it at my house and Mum's reaction made me glad we hadn't told Inspector Humphries about our near-death experience. She tutted and gasped her way through the item, making it hard for me and Graham to hear the details.

The police were trying to find the person who had tampered with the chocolates, but they hadn't got very far. It seemed that the stalker – dressed in the wizard outfit – had taken both the flowers and chocolates to the office of a local delivery firm. They'd paid in cash so they couldn't be traced.

"Didn't you think it was odd to be given items by someone in costume?" demanded the reporter.

"Fancy dress, I thought it was," the receptionist shrugged. "It's the party season; it's not unusual this time of year. We get all sorts in here."

"Putting poison into chocolates!" my mum exclaimed. "What will that stalker try next?"

"It's very often the case that killers have their own characteristic way of despatching their victims," Graham told her. "As long as poisoning remains his favourite method, Tiffany's relatively safe. She'll just have to watch what she eats."

"But what about you two?" Mum fixed me with an anxious frown. "I'm not sure you should carry on with this production. I'll bet your mum feels the same, Graham. Maybe I should give her a ring and see what she says."

Graham and I exchanged swift, horrified glances.

"We can't possibly let the rest of the cast down," Graham told her earnestly, surprising me with his streak of low cunning. "Not now. Our roles are pivotal – they couldn't train anyone else up in time. It's less than two weeks until opening night."

"We'll be fine," I said, backing him up for all I was worth. "The stalker's after Tiffany, not a pair of kids. We're not in any danger."

Mum looked from me to Graham, examining our faces. "OK," she conceded reluctantly. "I suppose you can't really leave everyone in the lurch."

She turned back to the television. The reporter was saying that the police were trawling through Tiffany's fan mail to see if they could match anyone's handwriting to the card on the chocolates.

Mum shook her head and sighed. "That will take them forever. And meanwhile that stalker's out there planning his next move. I just hope no one gets in his way. You can never tell how far a lunatic like that will go. Someone could get hurt."

"There are police all over the theatre, Mum. He's not going to get within a millimetre of any of us," I said cheerily. "Nothing bad's going to happen, I promise."

But sadly my optimism was totally and utterly misplaced. The very next day my mum's gloomy prophecy proved one hundred per cent accurate.

the tin man's axe

Graham and I arrived early for our next rehearsal. My mum was putting the finishing touches to a winter wonderland she'd created in the town centre and, as she was still fretting about the stalker, she insisted on giving us a lift. It was nice to be chauffeur-driven for a change, but it meant we got to the theatre ages before anyone else turned up. Everyone except Cynthia, and Maggie of course, who – as far as I could tell – never left the building.

Maggie greeted us with a broad smile. "You're keen," she said. "Nice to see such enthusiasm in a pair of youngsters."

She buzzed us through the security lock but before

we could disappear into the dark corridors she said, "Oh – could you find Cynthia and tell her that her son just phoned? He wants her to call him back."

"Yeah, OK."

"She'll be up in Tiffany's dressing room I should think. A dozen red roses just arrived so Cynthia took them up."

Suspicion gripped me and I turned to stare at Maggie. "More flowers?" I said sharply. "Who from?"

Maggie gave a throaty chuckle. "Peregrine. That man's gone completely daft over Tiffany if you ask me. Really, you'd think a chap of his age would know better. Still, you know what they say – there's no fool like an old fool."

"Are you quite certain they're from him?" Graham asked.

"Absolutely," said Maggie. "I called him to check. Nothing dodgy's getting past me, I assure you. Not after those chocolates."

Reassured, Graham and I went off to find Cynthia. But we'd barely set foot on the first set of stairs when I had the sensation that something was terribly wrong. The theatre was pretty much empty and I knew from experience that it was spooky when it was deserted, but this was worse than that. I couldn't quite put my finger on why the atmosphere was so unnerving.

My ears strained for the sounds of an intruder but I couldn't hear a thing. It wasn't until we neared the corridor where Tiffany's dressing room was that I realized it was the silence itself that was scaring me.

The slight squeaking of our trainers on the lino was the only noise in the building. Yet we knew that Cynthia was around somewhere: Maggie had said so.

So why couldn't we hear her?

In a blinding flash I remembered that Cynthia never did anything without singing to herself. You always knew exactly where she was and what kind of mood she was in. Cynthia's heart thumped along to a never-ending musical accompaniment: it came as naturally to her as breathing.

There had to be a reason for her silence. But it wasn't going to be a nice one.

As we rounded the corner we saw that Tiffany's door was wide open. Something bulky had wedged it firmly back against the wall. No. Not something. Someone.

My heart lurched horribly and Graham clutched my arm so hard that he left finger-shaped bruises all down it.

Cynthia's feet were sticking out across the corridor. She was face down and completely still. A smudge of blood in her hair showed where she'd been hit. Beside her the Tin Man's axe lay where her assailant had dropped it. She was still holding the dozen red roses Peregrine had sent to Tiffany.

Across the mirror – scrawled in red lipstick – were the words TIFFANY WILL DIE!

The window was wide open. The stalker must have climbed up the fire escape and lain in wait for Tiffany. Cynthia had surprised him when she opened the door. She must have seen his face. Perhaps she even recognized him. Or her. And so Cynthia had been killed. She'd been in the wrong place at the wrong time and paid the ultimate price for it.

Graham and I were about to go for help when there was a commotion behind us. Tiffany had arrived, along with her bodyguards. The burly pair of guardian angels swung into action at once, calling the police and cordoning off the area.

It was a narrow corridor and Graham and I were totally in the way. We backed off and headed towards the stage feeling shaken and upset. But before we left I had a good look at Tiffany. An expression of horror was on her face; her mouth was open, her eyebrows were raised, her hand was flat against her cheek, fingers outstretched. But she didn't look genuinely scared. Not like when Peregrine had told her to skip ahead to the last verse of her song.

"Are you sure?" asked Graham when I told him.

"Absolutely."

"That does seem like a most inexplicable reaction."

"You said it."

"I wonder what was going through her mind?" We looked at each other and fell as silent as Cynthia.

We didn't do any rehearsing that day. For a start, everyone was far too upset. Cynthia had been really popular, especially among the kids. She'd been kind to all of us so there were a fair few Munchkins who were crying inconsolably when we left the theatre. Once Cynthia's body had been taken away the police wanted to do a fingertip search of the entire building. We all got sent home. We weren't allowed back in for three days.

During our unscheduled break a big article about Tiffany appeared in a celebrity magazine. We were at my house having tea when Mum came in with it, and Graham and I fell on it as though we might find some clues to Tiffany's state of mind in there.

It wasn't very informative. All right, so we got to know what colour her duvet cover was (pink with her initials picked out in gold embroidery) and how her house was decorated (mostly pink and white) and what the garden looked like (mainly roses – pink ones, surprise, surprise), but it didn't say much about what made her tick.

The only remotely interesting thing was a photograph taken about five years ago before she was famous. When I looked at it closely my pulse began to race.

It was a picture of a group of teenagers dressed in *The Wizard of Oz* costumes. The caption said it was Tiffany's school production. The girl playing Dorothy was right in the middle, her face turned to the side as she grinned at one of the other actors. She was very pretty with thick black hair and high cheekbones. Cynthia would have said she had good bone structure.

It took me a while to find Tiffany. She was squeezed in to the far right-hand corner of the frame looking a lot younger and a little plumper. She was wearing a Munchkin outfit.

In a paragraph next to the photo Tiffany was quoted as saying, "We did a production of *The Wizard of Oz* at school when I was sixteen and I've loved it ever since. Getting the part of Dorothy now is like a dream come true."

"I wonder why she didn't get it back then?" I said.

"Who knows?" replied Graham. "Does it matter?"

I considered. "I think it does, yes. She's got a fabulous voice. How could they give the part to anyone else?"

"There's only one way to find out," said Graham. "Let's see what's on the Internet."

We switched on the computer. The name of the newspaper the photo had first appeared in was printed next to the image. By typing it into the search engine Graham found its site and then went through to the archives. It wasn't long before he'd printed out the article that originally went with the photo.

It was the kind of thing you get in local newspapers – listing all the kids who'd taken part and saying a few nice things about the show. A girl called Katie had been Dorothy and they'd written a few lines about her "shining performance" and how a "new star was born" and how she was "someone that would undoubtedly be gracing the West End stage in the future".

"Well they got that wrong," I said to Graham. "I don't recognize her. She obviously didn't make it as an actress."

Tiffany was mentioned too. "She made an excellent Munchkin, showing a flair for comedy that had us rolling in the aisles."

"That's odd," I said. "You don't think of Tiffany as being funny, do you?"

Graham didn't answer. He'd skipped to the bottom of the page and his eyes had grown wide with excitement. "Look!" he said.

I looked.

He was pointing at the last line. I read it out loud.

"After the curtain call the headteacher made a speech giving special thanks to the technical crew without whom, he said, none of this would have been possible: Ed Sawyer, Martin Smith, Gillian Riley and Jason Cotton."

"Jason Cotton?" I exclaimed. "Do you reckon that's our Jason?"

"Could be," Graham replied cautiously. "If it is, then that means he and Tiffany were at school together."

"So they might have known each other for years. But they never let on, did they? Tiffany never gave the slightest sign that she knew him when he first arrived. She looked right through him as if he wasn't there."

"Perhaps she didn't remember him," suggested Graham. "They might not have been friends."

"Maybe not. But surely in a school production like that you get to know everyone, don't you? They spend ages putting those things together. So she must be pretending not to. I wonder why?"

"I believe that the possibility of them ending up together in another version of *The Wizard of Oz* purely by chance is very unlikely," Graham said.

"So it must mean something?"

"It must," Graham decided.

The only problem was that neither of us could work out what it was.

ruby slippers

It took an awful lot of persuading before our parents would let us carry on with the show. In the end what swung it was the fact that the police had put the building under 24-hour surveillance. The stalker had slipped past them twice – they were determined he wasn't going to do it again. Graham recited a seemingly endless stream of statistics about muggings and street crime, and finally managed to convince both our mums that we were safer in the theatre than anywhere else in the country.

Not everyone shared Graham's powers of persuasion. When we were allowed back to work the population of Munchkinland had been decimated.

Graham and I didn't have a clue what Tiffany and Jason were up to but we were pretty sure that something was going on. We were careful – two people had died already and we didn't want to add ourselves to the grand total. But when we started rehearsing again – under the protective gaze of Daphne, Cynthia's replacement – we watched both of them like hawks.

By now everyone was feeling the pressure – we'd lost three days and opening night was just a week away. Peregrine solemnly informed his reduced cast that we would have to "work like demons" if we were going to be ready in time.

It was a major challenge, particularly with the number of policemen crammed into the building. They were guarding every window and every door. It was hard to move without falling over one.

"Which isn't much good if the stalker is one of us," I said to Graham. "I know Maggie said Peregrine is obsessed with Tiffany. But suppose he isn't?"

"What do you mean?"

"He could be pretending he's smitten to cover up how he really feels. Suppose he's trying to do away with her so he can claim on the theatre insurance?"

"As we know, money is frequently a motive in murder cases," opined Graham. "But Peregrine wasn't here in the building when Cynthia was killed. We were the first to arrive after she did."

"So Maggie said. But someone must have already been here to bash Cynthia. I know it looked like he'd climbed the fire escape. Yet it would be easy enough to hide in here overnight, wouldn't it?"

"Any one of us could have done that," said Graham.

"True," I conceded. I turned it over in my mind. "You don't reckon Jason might have something to do with it, do you?"

"If he knew Tiffany at school it's possible that he's been obsessed with her since then. But why would he choose to act on it now?"

"Cynthia said he'd been trying to get a job with the company for ages. Maybe he didn't have the chance before. Although he wasn't here when Geoff died," I pointed out.

"No. But he could have come up the fire escape and sneaked in to poison her tea."

"Good point. And I suppose he could have written that first note and stuck it on the theatre door," I mused.

"That wizard was too tall for Jason," objected Graham.

"He could have been wearing platform shoes or something," I suggested. "I didn't look at his feet, did you?"

"No," said Graham. "But if he did do all that he could have easily arranged the chocolates and flowers too."

"And bashed Cynthia."

"Yes," said Graham finally. "It's certainly a plausible theory. Jason could be our man."

Which wasn't a very reassuring thought considering our lives were literally in his hands. I mean, it was Jason who strapped us into our harnesses for the flying sequence. Jason who pushed the buttons that made our wings flap up and down. Jason who programmed the computer that controlled our trajectory. If the mood took him, Jason could send us crashing to the floor. We'd end up just like the Wicked Witch of the East. As flat as cowpats.

Graham and I were both tense and nervous but for almost a week nothing bad happened. Everyone was working their socks off, desperate to be ready for opening night.

On the morning of the dress rehearsal Mum needed to be at work extra early so once again she dropped us off at the end of the alley before any of the other kids had arrived at the theatre.

As usual, Maggie was at the stage door flanked by a couple of police officers. She waved to us as we approached.

I waved back but Graham didn't. He was frowning and I recognized it as a sign of Deep Thought.

"What is it?" I asked.

He pointed to the building. "There's the fire escape. If the stalker climbed that to poison Tiffany's tea, how did he get up there without Maggie noticing?"

"Someone must have distracted her. Delivered flowers or something. He could have sneaked past then."

"So he must have an accomplice," said Graham.

"But Maggie's not stupid. She'd have put two and two together. If she'd seen a stranger she'd have reported it to the police," I said thoughtfully. "So she must have been distracted by someone she already knew."

"Which means that one of the cast must have given him a hand…"

We reached the stage door and Maggie let us in, saying, "Hi you two! My, aren't you keen? You're the first in again. Peregrine should give you a prize for your enthusiasm!"

Graham and I headed towards the kids' dressing room. We were planning to just sit and wait for everyone else to arrive but over the intercom we could hear Tiffany up on stage, singing the opening bars of "Over the Rainbow".

"I thought Maggie said we were the first ones here," said Graham.

"Maybe she just meant we're the first kids to arrive," I replied, shrugging. I was more interested in the sweetness of Tiffany's song. "She's got an amazing voice. Magical." I suddenly remembered Cynthia's remark. "It's very consistent."

"Which is odd, when you think about it," said Graham.

"What do you mean?"

"Well in theory it ought to be impossible to reproduce exactly the same effect each time. The vocal chords change, you see, with variations in temperature and humidity. Strong emotion, diet, hot drinks – all sorts of things can affect the human voice."

Graham and I exchanged looks.

"Shall we go up and watch?" I said.

"Yes," said Graham slowly. "But we ought to be very careful."

So we were. We crept like mice through the corridors. By the time we tiptoed into the wings Tiffany's song had just finished. The last note was still hanging in the air but there was no one on stage but Jason.

Tiffany Webb had vanished. It was as if she'd clicked her ruby slippers and been magically transported home to Kansas.

the dress
rehearsal

Graham and I reversed without a word and crept back to the dressing room before Jason could see us. Once there, we shut the door firmly behind us and checked there was no one else around before we started discussing the possibilities.

"Maggie said we were the only ones here. Do you think she didn't know Jason had arrived?" I asked.

"But how could he have got past her?"

"I don't know," I said. "He could have stayed here last night, couldn't he? Perhaps he pretended to be working late. He might have told Maggie he'd lock up when he left. He's the technician – could he have his own set of keys?"

"That would explain an awful lot," replied Graham.

We both sat in silence while we considered the implications.

"But what about Tiffany? Do you think she was hiding just now?" I said.

"I suppose it's possible..." Graham didn't sound convinced.

"But not very likely."

"No... It's a big floor area," mused Graham. "We were there just as the song ended. She'd have had to sprint across the stage to get out of sight. And she doesn't look like a very fast runner to me."

"Plus we'd have heard her heels clicking across the floor."

Then we both said at the same time, "Why would she hide anyway?" We looked at each other, baffled.

"It's weird." I sighed, and Graham nodded. There was another long pause and then I added, "Suppose Tiffany wasn't there at all..." I talked slowly, speaking the ideas aloud as they came into my head, waiting for Graham to laugh or disagree with me but he didn't do either. Instead he nodded again. I continued. "If she wasn't there ... then she couldn't have been singing ... and if it wasn't her singing ... well, it certainly wasn't Jason. Was it?"

"I don't think so." Graham looked at me. "As far as I can see there's only one explanation that would fit all the facts."

"Which is?"

"It was a recording."

"A *recording*?" I echoed.

"It would explain the consistency of her performance," said Graham.

"No!" My mouth fell open as I took in what Graham was saying. "You think Tiffany's been miming?"

"It's a definite possibility. It's not uncommon for popstars to do it, especially for television appearances. Tiffany could have been miming all along."

"But … is that *allowed*? I thought it was supposed to be *live*. I thought that was the *point*." I felt quite indignant.

"Well … yes. Live theatre should be live. It would go against the Trade Descriptions Act if it wasn't."

"Do you think Peregrine knows?"

Graham shook his head. "I doubt that very much."

"Should we tell him?" I asked.

"We haven't got any proof," Graham said flatly.

We sat there for a bit, and then I exclaimed, "All that going from the beginning stuff! No wonder she looked so scared when Peregrine wanted her to skip to the end – it couldn't be done with a recording, could it?"

"Not without giving the game away."

"And that look up she does before she starts a song; that finger flick – she must have been giving Jason signals!" I exclaimed.

"Well, yes. I assume he is in on it. That would account for the strangeness of the sound system. I wondered from the beginning why he was using such complicated equipment – it didn't seem to make sense. But now it does. She's got what looks like two mikes. But one's a device to play the song and the other's an amplifier to make it sound like she's really singing. Jason must be using a remote control. It's very clever. He's been giving Tiffany her songs."

"Do you remember when we had to come back for my lunchbox and we heard that awful singing? Do you reckon that was her?"

"It could have been."

"That's probably why they said she was funny in the paper. If she was singing that badly in the school production they must have thought she meant it as a joke."

"But I don't get it," Graham said, suddenly exasperated. "How does all this fit in with the stalker? Why would Jason be helping Tiffany and then trying to kill her?"

We couldn't say any more to each other because the other kids had started to turn up. But later, in the dress rehearsal when we were sitting right at the back in our flower costumes, we managed to have a whispered conversation.

"OK," I said. "So if Tiffany's not really singing... Do you reckon Hannah noticed?"

"Maybe."

"That could be the reason for all those strange looks."

"Could be," agreed Graham.

We'd got to the bit of the song where we had to stand up and slowly twirl full circle three times, which was a tricky thing to do without getting our petals tangled so it was a while before we could say anything else. My mind was whirring furiously. We'd worked out what Tiffany and Jason were up to but that meant Jason couldn't be the stalker. He wouldn't be trying to kill the woman he was helping. Unless...

My next thought chilled me to the core. When we sat back down I said, "Graham, I'm scared."

"Why?"

"All this time we've been thinking the stalker was after Tiffany. But what if he wasn't?"

"What do you mean?"

"Well it was Geoff that died first, wasn't it? And then he got replaced. By Jason! What if killing Geoff was the whole point?"

Tamworth Library
24hr Renewal Line
Tel: 0345 330 0740

Items that you have checked out

Title: Dying to be famous
ID: 38014091256989
Due: 30/08/2022 23:59

Title: The black crow conspiracy
ID: 38014093145115
Due: 30/08/2022 23:59

Title: The wolves of Willoughby Chase
ID: 38014093716519
Due: 30/08/2022 23:59

Total items: 3
Account balance: £0.00
08/08/2022 15:20
Checked out: 3
Overdue: 0
Hold requests: 0
Ready for collection: 0
Messages:
X

Thank you for using Self Serve

General enquiries please call
00 111 8000
Thank you for visiting Your Library
w.staffordshire.gov.uk/libraries

"So what you're saying is that maybe Tiffany put the poison in her own cup to get rid of Geoff?" said Graham incredulously.

"Yes. And I think I saw her doing it!" I was practically exploding. "She put sweeteners in her tea. Suppose they weren't real ones? Suppose they were poison? Then all she had to do was accidentally-on-purpose spill Geoff's tea and give him her cup."

"That's why Maggie didn't see anyone come in," said Graham eagerly. "Tiffany was already there!"

"Yes!" I gasped. "She could have opened the door to the fire escape when she went to make a fresh cup of tea. She almost sprinted off the stage, do you remember? She'd have just had time to do it before her bodyguards caught up with her. Jason could have made those marks on the door frame when the building was empty – in the middle of the night or something – to make the police think it was an outside job. And that's why Cynthia didn't notice the door was open earlier. Ohmygod! Cynthia! She said that stuff about Tiffany's voice and Tiffany looked really angry. Maybe they thought she suspected something. Maybe they killed her too."

"They'd only have had to open the dressing room window to make it look like it was someone else," Graham agreed.

"Exactly."

We wafted woodenly to the left and then to the right not quite in time with the music. Tiffany set off for the Emerald City, ruby slippers skipping along the yellow brick road. We got to the end of the scene and there was a blackout when the inhabitants of Munchkinland had to leave the stage. But for a moment I couldn't move. I grabbed Graham and in the pitch darkness I hissed at him, "The chocolates!"

"You don't think...?" His voice trailed away to nothing.

"Yes. They weren't meant for Tiffany! No wonder she took the only toffee. It was a hard centre. She knew there wasn't any poison in it. She was trying to kill us!"

The lights came up then, catching me and Graham in their glare. The scenery had moved all around us and we were standing in the Scarecrow's field.

"Get off the stage!" shrieked Peregrine.

Graham and I fled, earning sour looks of disapproval from the Munchkins.

After that things went from bad to worse as far as Graham and I were concerned. We couldn't talk in the dressing room – there were too many people around. There wasn't any point even attempting to say anything to the police: we knew from past experience that they aren't very keen on listening to unproven crime theories from a couple of kids. So all we could do was get through the dress rehearsal in an agony of panic and anxiety. Our flying scene was dreadful: Toto wandered into the wrong place, and when we landed I ended up treading on his tail. He yelped and then sank his teeth into the Cowardly Lion, who swore very loudly. When we got hold of Dorothy and took off, Graham – in a sudden spasm of nervousness – jerked sideways and kicked the Tin Man's head as we flew past him so he started swearing too.

Peregrine was furious. "I have never seen such a shambles! That was appalling. Truly appalling," he berated us at the end of the rehearsal. "I hardly need remind you that we open tomorrow night. And right now this show is just not good enough. I expect everyone back here first thing tomorrow morning. We'll have to squeeze in another rehearsal. Two if necessary. It's our only hope."

So Graham and I felt tired and forlorn as well as in fear of our lives. We waited outside the theatre for Mum to pick us up, looking over our shoulders every five seconds to check that neither Tiffany nor Jason were sneaking up on us.

"So what do you think? Are we sure the stalker

doesn't exist?" I asked Graham. We looked at each other thoughtfully.

"It seems to be the most likely explanation," said Graham.

"He's been great publicity for the show, hasn't he? It sold out, didn't it? Maybe Tiffany and Jason dreamed him up in the first place as some sort of stunt. And then he was useful cover for getting rid of Geoff. And Cynthia. And us – if we'd eaten those chocolates."

"But why did they want to get rid of us?" wondered Graham.

"For the same reason they got rid of Cynthia – we saw too much. We heard Tiffany singing, didn't we? And you asked him about the sound equipment. It was enough to spook them into thinking we might work it out."

"Which we have," quavered Graham. "So will they try again?"

I breathed a deep sigh while I considered the answer. I surprised myself by suddenly feeling relatively safe. "You know, I don't think they will. Tiffany really, really wants this show to succeed – she's got a lot riding on it. They can't afford to do anything that would stop it going ahead now. It's opening night tomorrow: she'll be focused on that. They both will be. We should be safe enough as long as we keep our heads down."

So that was that. We had completely convinced ourselves that the stalker didn't exist but we were wrong. Because the very next day he struck again.

stage fright

Pretty much everyone in the theatre was riddled with nerves the day the show opened. Everyone, that is, except Tiffany.

She arrived that morning in a kind of happy glow because – according to the breakfast news – she'd just been offered a part in a major Hollywood film. She looked like she was walking on air. She was all beams and smiles to everyone, even the Munchkins. Jason, on the other hand, looked furious.

When we started the rehearsal one of Tiffany's microphones let out a terrible screech, then crackled and fizzled into nothing. Tiffany flicked a nail against it but it was totally dead.

Peregrine heaved a deep sigh and called for Jason, who came scurrying on to the stage.

Tiffany startled everyone by spitting furiously, "Did you do this deliberately?" I was amazed. I mean, they'd been so careful up until then not to give away the fact that they knew each other. But you don't speak to a stranger the way Tiffany just had to Jason.

He took a step back, darting a look at Peregrine before saying deliberately, "Of course not, Miss Webb."

I thought Tiffany was about to hit him but she pulled herself back when she saw the warning look in his eyes.

"Have you got a spare mike?" Peregrine asked Jason.

"No," Jason replied. "Miss Webb's microphone was … a special one… Non-regulation. It had its own speci-fication … a particularly sensitive decibel meter…"

"He's making it up," Graham whispered to me. "There's no such thing."

Peregrine started rubbing his forehead with his handkerchief. "Get another sent down from head office. Sort it out Jason. In the meantime we'll carry on without it."

Three things happened when he said that. Jason stared at Tiffany, his eyebrows raised as if he'd asked a question and was waiting for her answer. Hannah grinned from the wings, her black lipstick making her look like a witch. And Tiffany exploded.

"I'll strain my voice!" she screamed. "I refuse to work without a microphone! You can't possibly expect me to put up with these conditions." She stamped her foot like a toddler in a supermarket. I half expected her to lie down and start pounding the floor with her fists but instead she stalked off, ruby heels clicking across the stage as she made for her dressing room. Jason ran after her, and before they disappeared I heard her wail, "I'm going, I tell you. You can't stop me! No one can."

There was nothing Peregrine could do. He just stood there, aghast. We all did. The Munchkins were astounded to see a grown-up behaving like that. There was a long, dramatic silence.

And then Hannah stepped forward and said awkwardly, "Peregrine, do you want me to stand in…?"

Peregrine sighed despairingly and said, "It's kind of you, Hannah, but frankly, my dear, I've given up. Our fate is in the lap of the gods. We'll just have to keep our fingers crossed for this evening. I'm going to lie down in a darkened room and pray. I suggest the rest of you do the same."

Shepherded by Daphne, we had to file back to the dressing room, where we spent a long and agonizing day fretting about the coming performance. Everyone showed their terror in different ways – talking non-stop or not talking at all; cheeks flushed red, or faded to a sickly pale; bursting into tears or giggling hysterically.

Graham and I sat together, muttering.

"Who tampered with her microphone?" he asked. "Do you think it was Jason?"

"It can't have been! He wouldn't have helped her all this time just to stop now. It doesn't make sense," I replied. "Who else knew about her miming?"

"I don't know. Do you think Peregrine worked it out?"

"Might have. But why would he wreck his own show?" Then I remembered Hannah's face. "Maybe Hannah did it. I think she guessed ages ago that Tiffany was miming. And she did just offer to stand in for her, didn't she? Maybe she did it so she can play the part tonight."

"Well if it was Hannah who fixed the mike I hope she doesn't let on," said Graham gloomily. "I wouldn't fancy her chances if Tiffany finds out."

The trouble was, we couldn't really think straight. As the afternoon wore on we got more and more paralysed with stage fright. Graham looked like he was going to his own execution. I didn't think it was physically possible to feel so scared without actually passing out. I kept having to rush to the toilet and each time I stood up I felt faint and dizzy. It was horrible.

Half an hour before curtain up Elizabeth tapped on the dressing room door to give us our thirty-minute call. She continued down the corridor knocking on all the doors. Two minutes later she let out a blood-curdling scream.

Graham and I stared at each other. "Hannah!" we both shrieked.

But it wasn't Hannah who was lying dead.

When Tiffany hadn't answered the knock on her door, Elizabeth had pushed it open.

Tiffany was dead. And the writing on the mirror said: I Always Keep My Promises.

opening night

The police wanted to stop the show. For a while I wondered if Peregrine would let them and if he really had done away with Tiffany to collect the insurance money. But no, Peregrine was adamant the production would go ahead. We could hear him in the corridor saying urgently, "'The show must go on.' That's not a cliché, Inspector Humphries, it's the simple truth. It really cannot be cancelled."

"I'm sorry, sir," came the policeman's reply. "I can't allow…"

"There's a full house out there," Peregrine persisted. "If we don't proceed, the financial loss will break the company. As it is I've had to re-mortgage my house to cover our debts. An awful lot of jobs are dependent on this production's success. I beg of you. Please reconsider."

There was a long pause but eventually Inspector Humphries said, "Very well. You can go ahead. I'll take statements after the show."

Dizzy with shock and sick with nerves, we took our places.

Cynthia had been right, I noticed. Without her Goth make-up, Hannah – who'd had to get costumed up in five minutes flat – was very pretty. Very pretty and faintly familiar – I had the vague feeling that I might have seen her face somewhere before. And I wasn't the only one. When Jason – fingers shaking, lip trembling – tried to pin a microphone to her dress, she turned away and muttered, "I can manage without amplification, thanks."

She put a hand up as if to shield her face, but the movement just focused Jason's attention more closely on her. He stared, frowned and said, "Katie...?"

But he didn't get a chance to say any more because it turned out that Hannah was sick with nerves too. Literally. At that moment she spun round and threw up into the fire bucket, which brought their conversation to a sudden halt.

As for me, I was shaking so much that my petals were rustling like I was caught in a stiff breeze. I was deeply regretting having had anything at all to do with the production. I wanted to go home. Go to bed. Hide under the duvet and not come out until spring. I felt cold inside, as if I'd swallowed a ghost. Graham had lost the power to talk. He was swaying like his knees were about to give way.

But Hannah looked worse than both of us. I really couldn't see how she would be able to perform. Why was Peregrine putting us through it? Why hadn't he cancelled the show? What kind of sadist was he?

Peregrine made an announcement telling the packed theatre that Tiffany Webb was unable to perform and that the part of Dorothy would be taken by her understudy. This was answered by a howl of disappointment from the audience. Hannah was sick again.

But then something weird happened.

I'd read about actors whose fear disappears the moment they step out into the spotlight. As soon as the overture struck up, Hannah was suddenly transformed.

She stood up straight, flicked one of her plaits across her shoulder and smiled the kind of smile that fills everyone who sees it with a warm glow. She looked positively radiant. Star-like. When the curtains opened, she filled the stage with her magical presence.

Of course we'd never rehearsed with Hannah, but she was so good it wasn't a problem. It was like she picked up the whole cast in her arms and carried them along. You could feel the audience's love for her like great waves of warmth washing over the stage. She sang "Over the Rainbow" with the same familiar sad longing that we'd heard from Tiffany, but Hannah's voice seemed richer and fuller somehow. Maybe it was the difference between a recorded voice and a live one, I thought.

I was mesmerized. Captivated. Bewitched, just like everyone else. Even Graham wiped a tear from his eye. My brain was completely incapable of rational thought. So it wasn't until we got to the flying monkey bit that I realized who she was. We were holding her by the arms and were just taking off when the stage light caught the side of her face and lit up her profile. Suddenly I remembered the photograph of Tiffany's school production. Dorothy. Played by Katie somebody. It was her!

We soared up onto the platform. Down below us the non-flying monkeys were terrorizing the Cowardly Lion and the Tin Man, and beating up the Scarecrow while Toto yapped his head off. They were making so much noise that I knew no one in the audience would hear me if I spoke.

"You were at school with them!" I said. "Your name's not Hannah. It's Katie."

Which was possibly not the cleverest thing to say to a suspected murderess when you're wobbling on a narrow ledge ten metres above the stage. But Graham and I were both over-excited.

"The girl from the photo!" Graham pointed at her too. "No wonder you wore so much make-up – you've been in disguise, haven't you?"

"You tampered with Tiffany's microphone!" I accused her.

Graham gasped. "It was you, wasn't it? It was all you. You killed Tiffany!"

Hannah hadn't said a word but Graham and I started to back away because her pretty face was suddenly contorted with rage and hate.

"Tiffany deserved it!" Hannah spat. "I'm glad she's dead! She took everything from me!"

We were right on the edge of the platform and Hannah looked evil. She took a step towards us, and at that moment Graham and I turned and fled. There was nowhere to go but up the ladder and into the lighting grid.

We climbed through it with Hannah in pursuit.

Or so we thought. We couldn't really see much to be honest. She could have been escaping in the other direction for all we knew. I suppose we panicked. We were right in the middle of the grid when there was a lighting change. The big lanterns either side of us suddenly flared into life. They were hot as well as blinding and the shock made Graham lose his balance. He slipped. I tried to grab him and we both fell.

I thought we were done for: that we'd be splattered on the stage in front of a live audience. Our mums would never forgive us. But I forgot we were still in our harnesses.

We curved through the air in an elegant arc, kicking the Tin Man clean off his feet and knocking the straw out of the Scarecrow. The Cowardly Lion was sent spinning and poor little Toto weed all over the floor.

We were left dangling helplessly a metre above the stage in the full glare of the spotlights. The audience was in a confused uproar.

The Wizard of Oz had come to a sudden and dramatic end.

the grand finale

The safety curtain came down with a thud. Graham and I were still dangling a metre or so above the stage when everyone spilled out from the wings, including Inspector Humphries and Hannah.

"Arrest her!" I screamed, pointing at Hannah.

The inspector looked startled. "Why?"

"She's not called Hannah, she's called Katie. She's been in disguise," shouted Graham.

"She killed Tiffany!" I yelled.

"She just admitted it!" bellowed Graham.

"No, I didn't," Hannah said scathingly.

I looked at Graham to back me up but before he could speak Hannah explained, "I said she deserved to die. I didn't say I killed her."

"But you tampered with her microphone," I told her.

"Not guilty," Hannah answered firmly.

"But you knew Tiffany was miming, didn't you?" Graham chipped in.

There was a gasp followed by a chorus of disapproval. "Disgraceful!" said Peregrine. "Outrageous," agreed Timothy. "Appalling," grumbled Brad.

"Oh, yes, I knew all along she couldn't really be singing," said Hannah calmly. "I went to school with her: I knew full well she couldn't hit a note. I guessed she and Jason were going to work some kind of trick the minute I saw him. But then it was worse than I'd expected." She glared savagely at Jason. "That was the recording of the school production wasn't it, Jason? Cleaned up and edited, and then played through her own special microphone. Did you think you could get away with stealing my voice? She deserved what she got."

"Were you the stalker?" asked Graham.

"Of course not!" Hannah looked indignant. She was the picture of wounded innocence and I couldn't help but believe her.

"No – I think Jason and Tiffany did it," I said. "I reckon we were right about that. The letters, the chocolates – you did it between you, didn't you?"

All eyes were on Jason. Tears started to roll down his cheeks. He nodded slowly.

"So... Let me guess who did what," I said. "I think it was Tiffany's idea to get you to help. She knew she could only get away with singing if she was miming. So the first thing she needed to do was get rid of Geoff. That's why she invented the stalker. She made you dress up as the wizard, didn't she? No wonder I couldn't tell the difference between when she was acting and when she was being normal – she never *was* normal, was she? Her whole life was one big act!"

Jason looked around at the cast. "There was no stopping Tiffany when she wanted something," he mumbled sorrowfully. "She was so ambitious! She wouldn't let anyone or anything stand in her way. She arranged everything. She injected the chocolates with poison. She told me exactly how to kill Cynthia. I couldn't say no to her. She needed me, you see. How could I refuse? I've loved her for years – ever since we were at school together. And she told me she loved me too..." He looked suddenly baffled. "But that was wrong. She must have been lying. She can't have felt anything for me, or she wouldn't have..."

His voice trailed away to nothing.

"She was planning to go to Hollywood without you, wasn't she?" I asked.

"Yes! When the offer came through she said she wanted to go on her own. That a loser like me would only get in her way. I couldn't let her dump me just like that, not after everything I'd done for her. So I broke her microphone, just to show her how much she needed me. She couldn't manage alone, you see. I had to remind her."

"And what happened?" asked Graham. "Wouldn't she listen? Is that why you killed her?"

"I didn't kill her! I put a tranquillizer in her tea, that was all. I wanted to calm her down. She was so excited about the film offer, you see. Manic, almost. It was like she couldn't hear what I was saying. I only did it so she'd listen to me. It was just one pill!"

There was a sceptical sort of rumble from the cast, but I thought Jason was telling the truth. While he'd been talking I'd been revolving helplessly in my harness and my eyes came to rest on Rex. He looked strangely, unaccountably, massively *relieved*. I suddenly remembered that hasty, whispered conversation he'd had with Hannah when I was coming back from the toilets and a question popped out of my mouth.

"How do you and Hannah know each other?"

Rex smiled. Nodded. Stepped forward into the

spotlight. "Let me introduce you to a rising star. My beloved daughter, Katie Butler."

An astonished gasp rippled around the stage.

There was a hushed, expectant pause. Rex took a deep breath and opened his mouth to speak. "Jason didn't kill Tiffany Webb. But I rather think I might have done."

"No!" Hannah was aghast. "Daddy, you couldn't have! You didn't! I don't believe you!"

"I know, my darling, but I'm afraid it might be the truth." He faced the cast – an actor delivering his big speech to his hushed audience – and cleared his throat. "When I saw that Tiffany had been given the part of Dorothy I dreamt up a devious plot," he said. "I intended to prevent her performance right from the beginning. When I realized she had stolen my daughter's voice, I was doubly determined to stop her. Sadly, my grand scheme went a little awry at the end." He held out his hand to Hannah and she joined him at his side.

"I knew my daughter had star quality from the moment she was born, but until now she hasn't had quite the amount of luck she deserves – and one needs luck in this business as well as talent." He looked ruefully at Peregrine. "Sadly some directors like to have TV stars – names the public will recognize – to pull in the punters. Bums on seats, that's what it's all about these days. And so I hatched a cunning plan. I thought I'd arrange for Tiffany to have an accident at the eleventh hour – a sprained ankle, say, or a broken arm – something that would render her unfit to perform on opening night. Her understudy, stepping into her ruby slippers, would so dazzle the audience with her pure talent that she would become an overnight sensation. That was the only part of my scheme that actually worked. Darling, you were marvellous," he said, tenderly kissing Hannah on the cheek. "A triumph. Tonight will have launched your career. There's no looking back now."

"But why did you kill her?" I asked. "You didn't need to do that!"

"I didn't intend for Tiffany to die," Rex said with a sigh. "I had no idea the stalker wasn't genuine. There seemed something rather elegant about copying his methods. So instead of pushing her down the stairs as I'd planned, I elected to use pills. And later I daubed that message on the mirror to confuse the police, for which I now apologize." He nodded briefly at Inspector Humphries and then turned to Jason. "Murder was never my intention. I, too, simply wanted to put her temporarily out of action. I, too, slipped a pill into her tea. I suspect it was the combination of our actions that proved lethal. I thought I was solely responsible. I must confess I am a little relieved to know that we must share the burden of guilt."

He finished his speech and, folding his hands over his chest he gave a small, final bow. I almost started clapping.

There's not much to add, really. Both Rex and Jason were arrested and everyone else went home. Graham and I were left dangling on the empty stage and it took Elizabeth ages to work out how to get us out of the harnesses.

The old article in Hannah's local newspaper turned out to be right. *The Wizard of Oz* transferred to London after Christmas and she became a star of the West End stage.

Rex was prosecuted but he didn't get a very heavy prison sentence because he hadn't meant to kill Tiffany. Jason was dealt with more harshly because not only had he murdered Cynthia, he'd also been an accessory to Geoff's murder and the attempted poisoning of two children. Our mums weren't very pleased when they found out we'd kept that bit of information to ourselves.

When the Purple Parrot Theatre Company brought their production of *Joseph and the Amazing*

Technicolour Dreamcoat to the Theatre Royal, Graham and I were forbidden to even think about auditioning for it. We weren't exactly bothered about that. There are plenty of things we enjoy doing. But singing and dancing in a musical? We could live without it.

Zombies? Spooks?
Or just plain murder?

mondays
are
murder

zombies?
spooks?
or just plain murder?

tanya landman

My name is Poppy Fields. I never believed in
ghosts – until I stayed on a remote Scottish
island, and people started dropping dead
all over the place. Was a spirit taking revenge?
When Graham and I investigated, we began to
see right through it...

That's the way to do it!

dead funny

can you die laughing?

tanya landman

My name is Poppy Fields. I was dead excited about my first trip to America. But then people started getting themselves killed in really weird ways. Nothing made sense until Graham and I investigated, then the murders seemed to tie together as neatly as a string of sausages. A little *too* neatly...

On the trail of a murderer!

the
head is
dead

school won't kill you –
will it?

tanya landman

My name is Poppy Fields. When we
designed a murder mystery trail for
the school fayre, it was supposed to be a
bit of fun. But before long the head *was*
dead and Graham and I were hunting
down a real life killer.

Murder is a beastly business!

My name is Poppy Fields. Graham and I were first on the scene at a series of murders at the zoo, but who was behind them? We had to prowl around a bit to investigate – and what we saw was not pretty. How would we escape before we, too, became dead meat?

coming soon!